My Silly Granny

By TERRI LEEDOM

ILLUSTRATED BY MICHAEL PAUSTIAN

BookPress®

My Silly Granny is a children's book about dementia. It is designed to help young children understand why people they love may exhibit strange behavior, while also providing ideas for adults to help their children engage with and help the ones they love cope with this disease.

Granny loves having fun and playing games. She also enjoys sharing her snacks and favorite cookies.

Granny loves puppies and kitties! Playing music and singing to them makes her happy.

But sometimes Granny is
not very happy. There are
times when parts of her
brain don't want to work,
and she forgets how to do
things. It makes her sad,
and she feels embarrassed.

....I can't do this...I can't remember....

It's kind of like being in a thunderstorm and the lights go out. Sometimes the lights in Granny's brain go out. Later they come back on. The word doctors use to describe it is "dementia." They don't know how to fix it yet, so please be patient with Granny and remember, she can't help it.

There are times when Granny can't remember the right words to say, or how to say them. It makes her feel very frustrated and angry.

Granny gets confused and feels scared when she is not sure where she is or what she is doing.

Sometimes when days are too noisy and busy, Granny gets *really* confused. She just needs quiet time to sleep and let her mind rest. Do you want to be an angel and sing her a sweet lullaby?

There are lots of ways you can help Granny feel better. Tell her funny stories that will make her laugh. Ask her to tell you stories.

What did you like to do when you were a kid, Granny?

Granny will make you laugh when she pulls out her false teeth! When her own teeth got old, she had to replace them with new ones. Sometimes she gets silly with them!

When Granny has a bad day, music
can help her relax and have some fun.
You can giggle while
you wiggle!

You could bring a puppy or a kitty to visit Granny. Bring some snacks too, and you could have a picnic outside. That will give her joy!

Place Photo Here
of You and Your Silly Person

My name is
_____

My silly person is
_____

About the Author

Terri Leedom is a graphic designer and lives in West Des Moines, Iowa. As a child, she enjoyed drawing and writing stories. It wasn't until years later that she tapped into that creative spirit again and began writing short stories. When Terri's mother was diagnosed with dementia, she was inspired to write *My Silly Granny*, a light-hearted children's book based on her experiences.

Terri enjoys spending time with her family and romping with her granddogs. She also enjoys traveling, photography, music, dancing, and the Green Bay Packers. Terri feels most comfortable when she is outside connecting with nature. This is where she is most inspired.

To Granny

This book is dedicated to my mother, Donna. She was also a grandmother, great-grandmother, sister, aunt and friend, who had a spirited personality. In later years, she suffered from a type of dementia called Lewy Body Disease. It was quite frustrating for her, and for our family to understand her strange behavior. This disease taught us to live one day at a time. To laugh, to cry, to talk, to savor the moment and appreciate each day we had together, be it good or bad.

Published by: Bookpress Publishing • P.O. Box 71532, Des Moines, IA 50325 • www.BookpressPublishing.com

Publisher's Cataloging-in-Publication Data

Names: Leedom, Terri Ann, author. | Paustian, Michael, illustrator.
Title: My Silly Granny / written by Terri Ann Leedom; illustrated by Michael Paustian.
Description: Des Moines, IA: Bookpress Publishing, 2022. | Summary: A story designed to help young children understand why people they love may exhibit strange behavior, while also providing ideas for adults to help their children engage with and help the ones they love cope with this disease.
Identifiers: LCCN: 2022906796 | ISBN: 978-1-947305-41-0 | Subjects: LCSH Grandmothers—Juvenile fiction. | Dementia—Juvenile fiction. | Family—Juvenile fiction. | BISAC JUVENILE FICTION / Family / Multigenerational | JUVENILE FICTION / Health & Daily Living / Diseases, Illnesses & Injuries | Classification: LCC PZ7.1 .L44 My 2022 | DDC [E]–dc23

First Edition

Printed in the United States of America

10 9 8 7 6 5 4 3 2 1